The Biggest Cookie in the World

By Linda Hayward
Illustrated by Joe Ewers

Featuring Jim Henson's Sesame Street Muppets

A Random House PICTUREBACK® READER

Random House/Children's Television Workshop

Library of Congress Cataloging-in-Publication Data:
Hayward, Linda. The biggest cookie in the world. (Pictureback reader) SUMMARY: Waiting for his cookies to bake in the oven, Cookie Monster daydreams about his favorite subject. ISBN: 0-394-84049-6 [1. Cookies—Fiction. 2. Baking—Fiction. 3. Monsters—Fiction] I. Ewers, Joe, ill. II. Title. III. Series. PZ7.H31495Bi 1989 [E] 88-36247

Manufactured in the United States of America. 1 2 3 4 5 6 7 8 9 10

Some butter.
Some sugar.
Some eggs.
Some flour.

What time is it, Cookie Monster?

Time to make cookies!

Time to mix.

Time to roll.

Time to bake.

Dum-de-dum.
Time to wait.

Time to think about
the BIGGEST cookie
in the world.

Some butter.

Some sugar.

Some eggs.

Some flour.

Time to mix.

Time to roll.

Time to bake.

Cowabunga!
Time to eat.

Oh, oh.
Something is burning.

Time to start over.